# I DID IT, I'M SORRY

Caralyn Buehner   *Pictures by* Mark Buehner

Dial Books for Young Readers  New York

*A key to the correct answers can be found on the last page.*
*Also concealed in the pictures are many little animals—*
*see how many you can find. One clue: There's a bee, cat, rabbit,*
*and tyrannosaurus hidden in each picture, plus other animals*
*such as whales and gorillas scattered throughout.*

Published by Dial Books for Young Readers
A member of Penguin Putnam Inc.
375 Hudson Street
New York, New York 10014

Text copyright © 1998 by Caralyn Buehner
Pictures copyright © 1998 by Mark Buehner
All rights reserved
Designed by Nancy R. Leo
Printed in Hong Kong
First Edition
1 3 5 7 9 10 8 6 4 2

Library of Congress Cataloging in Publication Data
Buehner, Caralyn.
I did it, I'm sorry/by Caralyn Buehner; pictures by Mark Buehner.
p.   cm.
Summary: Ollie Octopus, Bucky Beaver, Howie Hogg, and other
animal characters encounter moral dilemmas involving such virtues as honesty,
thoughtfulness, and trustworthiness. The reader is invited to select the
appropriate behavior from a series of choices.
ISBN 0-8037-2010-6 (trade).—ISBN 0-8037-2011-4 (lib.)
[1. Conduct of life—Fiction. 2. Animals—Fiction.
3. Literary recreations.] I. Buehner, Mark, ill. II. Title.
PZ7.B884Iam 1998 [E]—dc21 97-10216 CIP AC

*The art for this book was prepared by using oil paints over acrylics.*

With love to our children
C.B. and M.B.

D<small>O YOUR WORDS AND ACTIONS HELP, OR HURT?</small>
Here is a quiz to help you find out. Choose the letter of
the answer you think is best. Then look at the picture and
see if you can find that same letter hidden in the picture. If
you can, you picked the right one!

Let's see how you do!

In the jungle where Harlan Monk lives, it is the law that
no one may swing over the water from a mava-mava vine.
But Harlan does.

I can take care of myself, Harlan thinks. That law is as
outdated as the old fogeys who worry about it.

Soon several of Harlan's friends are swinging on mava-
mava vines too. But one day the mava-mava vine breaks,
and Harlan falls into the dark lagoon below.

Too bad that Harlan never learned:

   a. How to sing "Jungle Bells."
   b. Mava-mava beans make your mouth purple.
   c. Laws and rules help keep us and others safe.

Ollie and Oscar Octopus are playing an exciting game of Tentacle Tag when Mom calls Ollie to come and watch for dinner. Ollie is having a lot of fun and doesn't want to stop.

What should Ollie do?

a. Quickly obey Mom.

b. Tag Oscar a few more times.

c. Sing a few verses of "Only an Oyster Would Think You're a Pearl."

"Barnabus," says Mama Batt, "I need you to look after the baby while I am gone tonight."

"Okay," agrees Barnabus. He doesn't mind baby-sitting. But after his mother leaves, four of his friends fly up.

"Come on, there's a tree-ball game starting!" they tell him.

Barnabus *loves* to play tree ball, and his little sister will just hang here all night anyway. Barnabus would really like to go. But he *did* tell his mom he would stay home with the baby, so he should:

  a. Play tree ball.

  b. Be dependable and stay with his little sister.

  c. Go see *Bat on a Hot Tin Roof* at the movie theater.

While Randy is racing to Rhoda's one day, he runs across Rudy's red rubber radio. Randy is a responsible raccoon, so he reaches for Rudy's red rubber radio and resolves to:

a. Rinse Rudy's red rubber radio in the river.

b. Run over Rudy's red rubber radio repeatedly.

c. Return the red rubber radio to Rudy right away.

Even though she studied hard for this test, Ima Scalebody can't remember where sea horses graze. Ima thinks that Lynn Finn will know the right answer, and she is tempted to peek and see what Lynn has written down. What should Ima do?

a. Tell her teacher she is feeling seasick.

b. Take the bait, and copy Lynn's answer.

c. Sink or swim on her *own*.

Bucky Beaver has been happily chiseling the table legs with his new front teeth. When Mother brings dinner in, she is horrified!

"Who did this?" Mother demands.

Bucky looks up and says:

a. "Gee, Mom, I have no idea. We must have termites."

b. "Oops! Gotta run! I'm late for my dam-building class!"

c. "I did it. I'm sorry."

Buzzer and Annoya McFly have brought their younger brother Pester to Frontier Cow Pies for an all-you-can-eat buffet. A sign at the door reads:

5 AND UNDER
EAT FREE

"Listen," Annoya says to Pester, "you're only six, and not very big. Tell them you're five."

But all night they feel uncomfortable, and don't even enjoy their pies. They are all sorry that they forgot:

a. Honesty is the best policy.

b. The food is better at Carcass's.

c. To bring the Pepto-Buzzmol.

Howie Hogg always enjoys playing with the Straw, Sticks, and Bricks set whenever he goes to Grandma's. He makes some wonderful houses, but all too soon it is time to go. Before he leaves, Howie should make sure to:

a. Tweeze his snout hairs.

b. Clean up his mess.

c. Tell Grandma she lives in a pigsty.

Flora Flamingo and her friend Flavio are leaving the market on a hot summer day. Flora eats her candy, dropping the wrappers as she goes. Then she drinks her soda and tosses the cup behind her.

Flavio always thought Flora was smart, but now, as he follows behind her picking up her garbage, he thinks she is pretty dumb because:

a. She will get cavities.

b. She wants to be a lawn ornament when she grows up.

c. Littering makes the world uglier for *everyone*, even Flora.

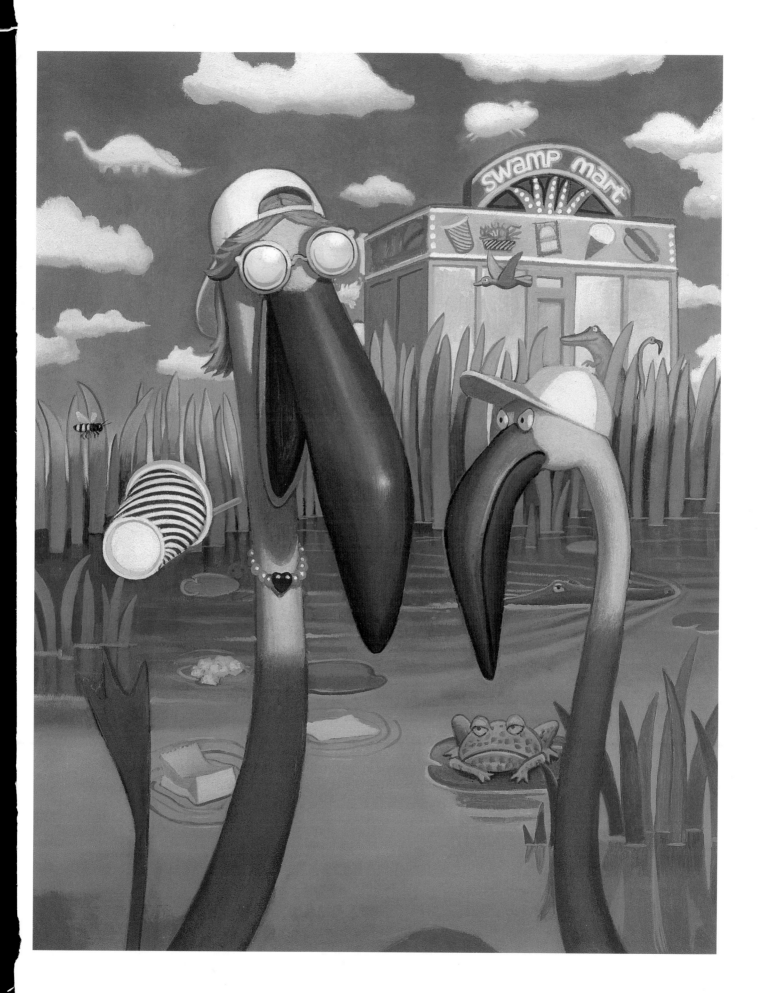

Pola Bear is telling Pawla about the seal hunt. He wants to boast about how dangerous and exciting it was, so he uses a lot of swear words to impress her. Then he tells a dirty joke.

"That does it!" growls Pawla, stalking off. "You've really spoiled a good story!"

Someone needs to tell Pola that:

a. He should try again in the moonlight.

b. Pawla prefers pink polish on her paws.

c. Good language doesn't bother anyone, but bad language often does.

Cory, Carmike, and Carla have been hanging out on the same dune all afternoon.

"I'm bored," says Carla. "Let's go to the oasis and trample some plants. Let's spit in the water."

"Yeah!" cries Cory. "Then let's stomp on that nomad, and chew up his tent!"

But Carmike is shaking his head.

"No way, guys," he says. "That is totally uncool."

Carmike knows:

a. Cool kids and camels never sneeze in a sandstorm.

b. Cool kids and camels respect other people, their rights and property.

c. "Cool" means you never have to say you're hairy.

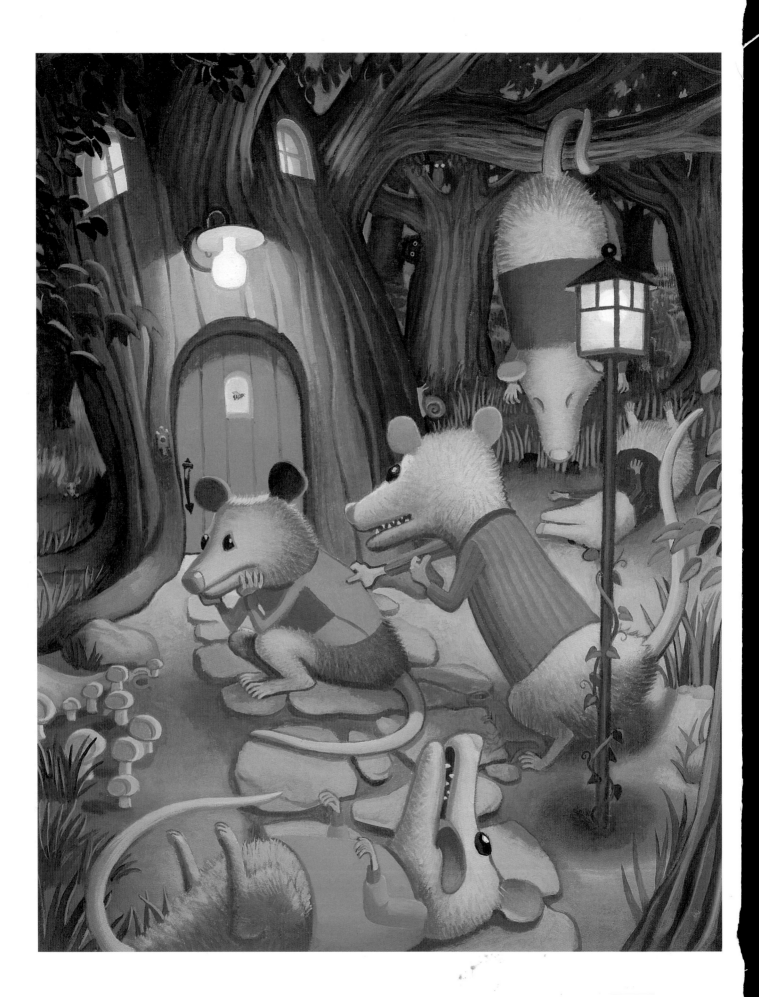

Everyone is having a lot of fun at the annual Possum Pajama Party—everyone, that is, except Perry. He is just not very good at Pin the Tail on the Tree Slug, and he never knows when to sit during Musical Rocks. Now it's time to play Dead, and no one wants Perry to be on *their* team!

Peter can see that Perry feels bad, and he wants to help him enjoy the party, so he says:

a. "Come on, Perry! Hang over here with me! I really
   need you on my team!"

b. "Why don't you crawl back in your mama's pouch?"

c. "There once was a possum named Perry,
   Whose tail had always been hairy.
   The fur wouldn't grip,
   So he always would slip,
   And hanging with Perry was scary!"

Rateesh watches nervously as Greenmeat, Fungusto, Rottenburger, and Diseasa begin eating lunch.

I'll never make any friends, Rateesh thinks. No one ever talks to me. Besides, they're all so *different*. I want to move back to Dumpsterville.

Just as a tear is about to roll down his nose, Rateesh remembers what Grandma Refusa used to say. Quickly he opens his lunch pail, takes out some old cheese, and divides it up.

"Do you guys want some cheese?" Rateesh offers.

"Sure!" The others gather around. "Thanks!"

"Here!" says Rottenburger. "Have some cake."

"I have some crusty tuna," says Diseasa.

Rateesh feels warm inside and is glad he remembered:

  a. To shave his tail.

  b. *Ratman* is on TV tonight.

  c. Kindness begins with *me*.

All the other sheep have been dyeing their wool bright purple. Before that it was shearing the wool off their necks and having cow tattoos! Sheila doesn't like purple, or feeling bare. It takes a lot of courage to be different, but Sheila isn't afraid because she knows:

a. The grass is always greener with the wool pulled over your eyes.

b. If you follow the herd, you might end up in the wrong place! Be who you really want to be!

c. A wolf tattoo would look better.

How did you do? Did you choose the right letters? Good for you! There are a lot of good things one person can do! Remember:

> Never lie for a pie like Pester McFly,
> Speak words that are clean and kind,
> Think of others (like Peter the Possum),
> Return any items you find.
> Quickly obey your mom and dad,
> Follow their jungle rule,
> And you will discover, like Carmike,
> The very best way to be cool!

# ❧ Answer Key ❧

**Harlan Monk:** The answer "c" is on the stone near Harlan's arm.

**Ollie Octopus:** The answer "a" is next to the curl in Ollie's nearest tentacle.

**Barnabus Batt:** The answer "b" is in the middle of the shoreline.

**Randy Raccoon:** The answer "c" encircles the left knob of the radio.

**Ima Scalebody:** The answer "c" is around the bubble under the desk of the red fish.

**Bucky Beaver:** The answer "c" is in a tree ring on the stool.

**Pester McFly:** The answer "a" is on a plate on the waitress's tray.

**Howie Hogg:** The answer "b" is on the straw house.

**Flora Flamingo:** The answer "c" is on the lily pad near Flora's necklace.

**Pola Bear:** The answer "c" is around Pola's ear.

**Carmike Camel:** The answer "b" is in the palm tree to the right of the tent.

**Peter Possum:** The answer "a" is between two mushrooms near the stone by Perry.

**Rateesh Rat:** The answer "c" is in a hole in the cheese.

**Sheila Sheep:** The answer "b" is near the rainbow-colored patch of wool on one sheep's forehead.

In addition, there are hidden pictures of a bee, cat, rabbit, and tyrannosaurus in every illustration. Scattered throughout are pictures of other animals such as whales and gorillas.